Laila Perseveres

Written By: Sasha Wright

This book is dedicated to:

Every child and inner child
that wants to give up when
something seems too hard,
I dare you to push through
to the end! The reward will
be worth the effort!

Laila Perseveres

Written By: Sasha Wright

It was only Tuesday and Laila was already frustrated with the amount of school work she had to do each day.

Laila looks around and notices the other students are already finished and are playing on their iPads. She thinks to herself, "I'll just turn my work in and get on my iPad because this is just too difficult."

Just then, Byron approaches Laila and asks her if she wants to challenge him on Math Wizards on the iPad.

Laila accepts the challenge and
leaves her uncompleted work
at her seat.

While playing Math Wizards, Laila gets frustrated and quits in the middle of the game. She accuses Byron of cheating because he was getting all of the answers right.

During writing time Laila decided to write about basketball. She loves basketball but she hates writing. Her teacher, Mr. Lewis, told her to write about something she loves.

Laila thought to herself…"Mr. Lewis wants me to write about something I love, but I don't know how to spell a lot of words." She started to write but gave up after she couldn't spell the word dribble.

Laila put her head down and began to cry.

Laila's friend Karla noticed she was crying and asked, "Laila what's wrong? Why are you crying?"

Laila cried, " 2nd grade is just too hard! I want to quit 2nd grade and just stay home with my dog Rocky."

Karla looked Laila in the face and said, "Quitting is not an option. You have to ask for help when things are hard."

Laila sat up and raised her hand

to ask Mr. Lewis for help.

Mr. Lewis came over to Laila and noticed she had not completed her morning work nor her writing again today.

Laila looks up at Mr. Lewis with tears in her eyes and said, "Mr. Lewis, Karla says I should ask for help when things get hard and right now writing is really hard. I just want to quit."

Mr. Lewis tells Laila, "Karla is absolutely correct and a great friend for encouraging you to make a positive choice. You should always ask for help when you need it." As he looks at her work on her desk he sighs, "It looks like you have a lot of incomplete work."

Laila nods her head and tells Mr. Lewis, "The work is just too hard and sometimes it is just easier to move on to something else."

Mr.Lewis says, "I completely understand. But easier doesn't always mean better. When something is hard but good for you, you must persevere and see it through. It doesn't have to be perfect and it doesn't have to be right...it just needs to be your best."

Laila asks, "But what is persevere?" Mr. Lewis shares, "In 1892 a beautiful baby girl was born that looked a little like you. Her name was Bessie Coleman. She grew up to face many challenges. One of her biggest challenges was becoming a pilot. Bessie Coleman wanted to fly airplanes but because she was a woman and because she was black, it was very hard. You see, women pilots and African American pilots were unheard of. Bessie had to learn the french language, raise money, and move to France to learn how to fly airplanes. In 1921 she received her international pilot license. Although it was hard and it would have been easier to stay home and work with her brothers, Bessie persevered and achieved her goal."

Laila was astonished that someone like her could accomplish such a dream. She made a deal right then, "Mr. Lewis, I won't quit or give up any more. Like Bessie Coleman, I will persevere and do my very best on all of my work."

Mr. Lewis taught Laila a phrase to help her persevere. He wrote it on a sticky note and stuck it to her desk. The note read: "I must get done, I must get through, I'll **PERSEVERE** and see it through!"

Laila's Challenge:

1. Think of something you have a hard time doing.
2. Make a plan and follow through.
3. Encourage a friend to do the same!

66900189R00027

Made in the USA
Middletown, DE
16 March 2018